P9-DFH-269

SIDE BY SIDE
LADO A LADO

The Story of
Dolores Huerta *and*
Cesar Chavez

La Historia de
Dolores Huerta *y*
César Chávez

by **Monica Brown** *illustrated by* **Joe Cepeda**

translated by **Carolina Valencia**

An Imprint of Harper Collins *Publishers*

I'd like to thank Lori de Leon and Dolores Huerta for their support and feedback during the writing of this book. I am filled with gratitude and admiration. —Monica Brown

Quisiera dar las gracias a Lori de León y a Dolores Huerta por su apoyo y por la información que me proporcionaron durante el desarrollo de este libro. Las admiro mucho a ambas y les agradezco su generosidad. —Monica Brown

Side by Side / Lado a lado: The Story of Dolores Huerta and Cesar Chavez / La historia de Dolores Huerta y César Chávez

Printed in the United States of America.

For information address HarperCollins Children's Books, a division of HarperCollins Publishers, 195 Broadway, New York, NY 10007. www.harpercollinschildrens.com

Joe Cepeda created the full-color illustrations using oil over acrylic, collage, and pencil on illustration board.

Joe Cepeda realizó las ilustraciones a todo color utilizando óleo sobre acrílico, collage y lápiz en papel ilustración.

Library of Congress Cataloging-in-Publication Data is available.
ISBN 978-0-06-122781-3 (trade bdg.)

Typography by Amy Manzo Toth
17 18 PC 10 ❖ First Edition

To Isabella, who is already working to make the world a better place

A Isabella, que ya comenzó a laborar para mejorar el mundo

—M.B.

For the children of the San Joaquin Valley

Para los niños del Valle de San Joaquín

—J.C.

In New Mexico, there lived a little girl named Dolores who talked so fast that her grandfather once said, "Dolores, you must have seven tongues!"

Había una vez en Nuevo México una niña llamada Dolores que hablaba tán rápido, que una vez su abuelo le dijo:

—¡Dolores, parece que tuvieras siete lenguas!

Many miles away in Arizona, there lived a little boy named Cesar who was a very good listener. Cesar listened to his mother cry when his family lost its home and they had to become migrant farmworkers.

A muchas millas de distancia, en Arizona, vivía un niño llamado César que sabía escuchar muy bien. César escuchó llorar a su mamá cuando la familia perdió su casa y tuvieron que volverse campesinos migratorios.

When Dolores was a girl, she moved to California with her mother and brothers. She joined the Girl Scouts and worked to raise money for soldiers fighting in World War II.

Cuando Dolores era niña, se mudó a California con su mamá y sus hermanos. Allí se hizo miembro de las Girl Scouts y ayudó a recaudar dinero para los soldados que luchaban en la Segunda Guerra Mundial.

Cesar's family moved to California to follow the crops and work in the fields. Although he had to drop out of school to work, Cesar always had a book under his arm.

La familia de César se mudó a California para trabajar en los campos, de cosecha en cosecha. Y aunque él tuvo que dejar la escuela para ponerse a trabajar, César siempre llevaba un libro bajo el brazo.

From her mother, Dolores learned to think of others. When poor farmworker families had no place to sleep, Dolores's mother would let them stay at her hotel for free.

De su mamá, Dolores aprendió a pensar en los demás. Cuando las familias campesinas pobres no tenían dónde dormir, la mamá de Dolores las dejaba quedarse en su hotel gratis.

Life for Cesar's family was difficult. All day they bent over in the hot sun picking lettuce, strawberries, and grapes. There was never enough water to drink out in the fields.

La familia de César tuvo una vida difícil. Se pasaban el día entero agachados a pleno sol recogiendo lechugas, fresas y uvas. Y en los campos nunca había suficiente agua para beber.

Dolores grew up and became a teacher. She saw the farmworker children come to school cold and barefoot, too hungry to learn as well as they could.

Cuando Dolores creció, se hizo maestra. Ella vio a los hijos de los campesinos llegar a la escuela descalzos, con frío, y con tanta hambre que les costaba trabajo aprender.

When Cesar grew up, he and his friends were hurt by dangerous tools and had mean bosses who sprayed the plants with poisons that made the farmworkers sick.

Cuando César creció, él y sus amigos se lastimaron al trabajar con herramientas peligrosas y tuvieron patrones crueles, que rociaban las plantas con sustancias venenosas que enfermaban a los campesinos.

Then something special happened. Dolores and Cesar met.

Dolores saw that Cesar had great faith. His dreams would bring hope to thousands of farmworkers.

Cesar saw that Dolores had great courage. She would stand up and fight for what was right.

Side by side, Dolores and Cesar began their journey.

Entonces, sucedió algo muy especial. Dolores y César se conocieron.

Dolores vio que César tenía mucha fe y que sus sueños darían esperanza a miles de campesinos.

César vio que Dolores era muy valiente y que sería capaz de luchar por lo que era justo.

Lado a lado, Dolores y César comenzaron a recorrer el mismo camino.

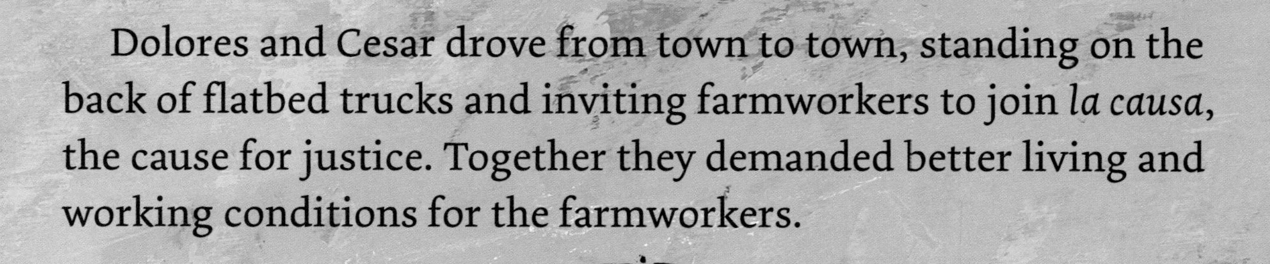

Dolores and Cesar drove from town to town, standing on the back of flatbed trucks and inviting farmworkers to join *la causa*, the cause for justice. Together they demanded better living and working conditions for the farmworkers.

Dolores y César fueron de pueblo en pueblo. Se paraban en las plataformas de los camiones e invitaban a los campesinos a unirse a la causa a favor de la justicia. Juntos exigieron mejores condiciones de trabajo y de vida para los campesinos.

Cesar and Dolores asked people to stop buying grapes from California because the poisons the growers used there were making the workers sick. People listened, and the grapes rotted on the vines.

The farmworkers won! They got a safer place to work, and the grapes became safer for people to eat.

César y Dolores le pidieron a la gente que dejara de comprar uvas de California, pues las sustancias venenosas que los dueños de los cultivos usaban allí hacían que los campesinos se enfermaran. La gente los escuchó y las uvas se pudrieron en los viñedos.

¡Los campesinos ganaron! Consiguieron que el lugar donde trabajaban fuera más seguro y que la gente comiera uvas más saludables.

Cesar led men, women, and children on a 340-mile march to demand that workers get paid enough to live on. They arrived in Sacramento, California, on April 10, Dolores's birthday. Dolores gave an amazing speech, and the people were heard! The growers signed a contract with the workers, giving them better pay for their hard work.

It was time for the farmworkers to share in the harvest!

César encabezó una marcha en la que hombres, mujeres y niños se desplazaron 340 millas para exigir que el pago de los trabajadores fuera suficiente para poder vivir. Llegaron a Sacramento, California, el 10 de abril, día del cumpleaños de Dolores. Dolores pronunció un discurso increíble y ¡al fin se escuchó la voz del pueblo! Los dueños de los cultivos firmaron un contrato y ofrecieron a los trabajadores un salario más justo por el duro trabajo que realizaban.

¡Por fin, los campesinos recibían su parte de la cosecha!

Though they each had a large family, little food, and no money, when Dolores and Cesar sat down at Cesar's kitchen table, they always looked for ways to make the world a better place. "If we don't help the farmworkers," Cesar asked Dolores, "who will?"

Aunque los dos tenían una familia numerosa, poca comida y nada de dinero, cuando Dolores y César se sentaban a la mesa en la cocina de César, siempre buscaban formas de mejorar el mundo.

—Si nosotros no ayudamos a los campesinos —le decía César a Dolores—, ¿quién lo hará?

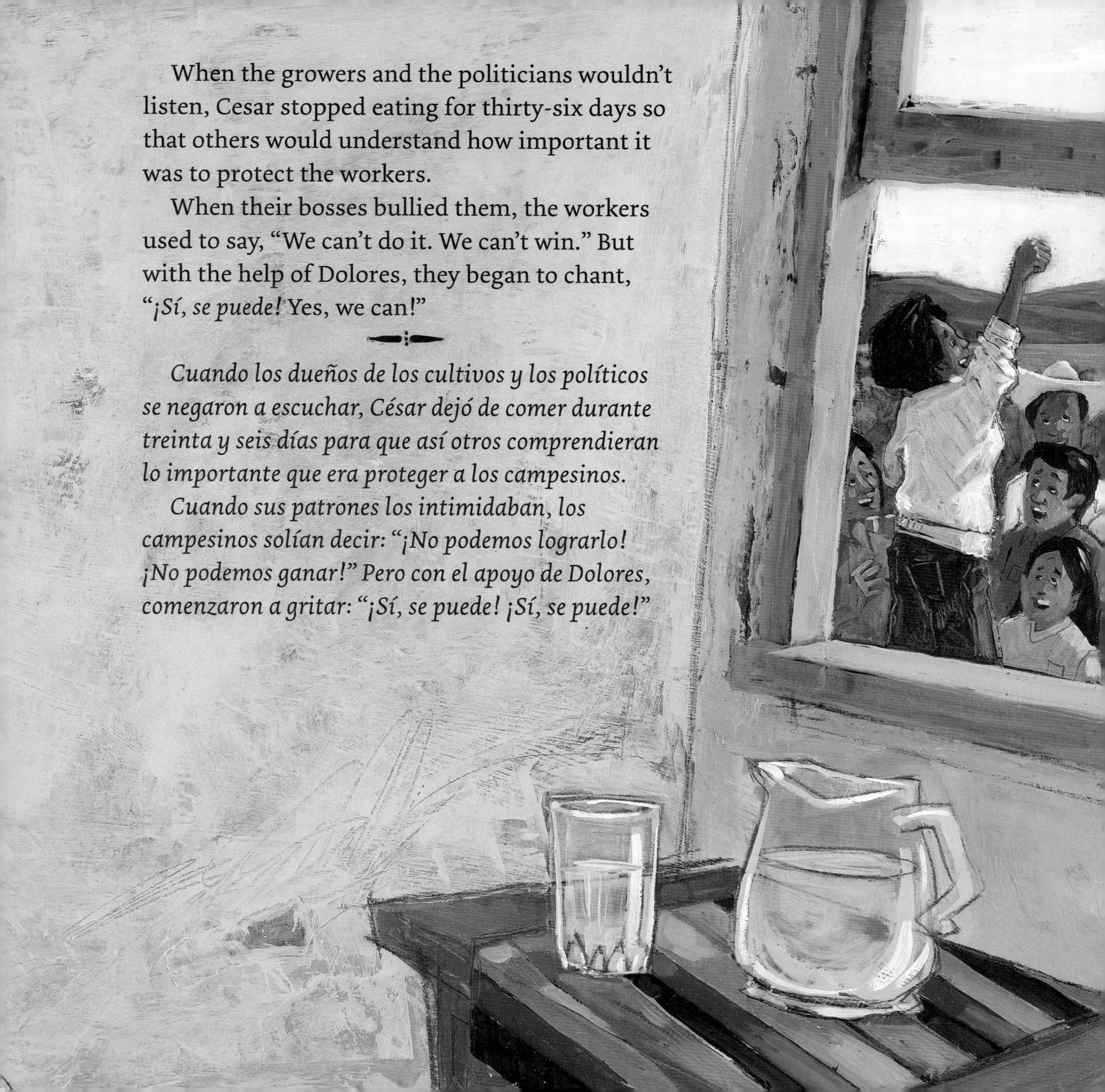

When the growers and the politicians wouldn't listen, Cesar stopped eating for thirty-six days so that others would understand how important it was to protect the workers.

When their bosses bullied them, the workers used to say, "We can't do it. We can't win." But with the help of Dolores, they began to chant, "*¡Sí, se puede!* Yes, we can!"

Cuando los dueños de los cultivos y los políticos se negaron a escuchar, César dejó de comer durante treinta y seis días para que así otros comprendieran lo importante que era proteger a los campesinos.

Cuando sus patrones los intimidaban, los campesinos solían decir: "¡No podemos lograrlo! ¡No podemos ganar!" Pero con el apoyo de Dolores, comenzaron a gritar: "¡Sí, se puede! ¡Sí, se puede!"

For thirty years, Dolores and Cesar worked and listened and talked and marched—side by side.

Dolores and Cesar worked to help families stay together. They fought to pass the immigration act of 1986 that helped more than a million immigrants become United States citizens.

Dolores and Cesar had many victories because they knew that, together, all things were possible.

Durante treinta años, Dolores y César trabajaron y escucharon y hablaron y marcharon, lado a lado.

Dolores y César lucharon para ayudar a las familias a permanecer unidas. Lucharon por la aprobación de la ley de inmigración de 1986 que ayudó a más de un millón de inmigrantes a convertirse en ciudadanos estadounidenses.

Dolores y César obtuvieron muchas victorias porque sabían que juntos, todo era posible.

In 1993, Cesar passed away, and Dolores and the farmworkers marched to honor him.

César murió en 1993. Dolores y los campesinos organizaron una marcha en su honor.

Dolores still works and marches for justice for the poor. And she is not alone. The spirit of Cesar Chavez is with her, by her side.

Dolores todavía trabaja y participa en marchas a favor de la justicia para los pobres. Y no está sola, el espíritu de César Chávez está con ella, a su lado.

SI
SE
PUEDE
USTICE

A Note for Parents and Teachers

Both Dolores Huerta and Cesar Chavez learned about injustice at a very early age, and both decided to do something about it. Dolores Huerta was born in 1930 in the mining town of Dawson, New Mexico. Her parents, Alicia Chavez and Juan Fernandez, were her first activist role models. Nine hundred miles away, in Yuma, Arizona, Cesar Chavez was born in 1927, the child of farmworkers who lost their home because they couldn't afford to pay taxes.

Dolores and Cesar met while working with Fred Ross and the Community Service Organization, an activist group in California. In 1962 they established the National Farm Workers Association to organize the migrant farmworkers of California. It was the beginning of a long and powerful collaboration. In 1967, Dolores and Cesar cofounded the United Farm Workers union. Cesar became president of the union, and Dolores became the vice president. In that same year, Cesar Chavez led a historic march from Delano, California, to the steps of the capitol in Sacramento, where thousands of supporters joined him on Easter Sunday. Dolores organized the National Grape Boycott and was instrumental in the passing of the immigration act of 1986, which allowed more than a million workers to become United States citizens. Together they celebrated many victories in their nonviolent struggle for social justice—fighting to secure health benefits, farmworker clinics, pensions, and collective bargaining for the farmworkers.

It was in Phoenix, Arizona, that Dolores Huerta first spoke the famous words "*¡Sí, se puede!*" While speaking to a group of workers who kept saying, "We can't organize the workers here. We can't. *¡No se puede!*" Dolores responded, "*¡Sí, se puede!* Yes, we can!" Finally the workers listened and had faith.

Cesar Chavez once said, "When the man who feeds the world by toiling in the fields is himself deprived of the basic rights of feeding, sheltering, and caring for his own family, the whole community of man is sick."* Cesar Chavez and Dolores Huerta dedicated their lives to healing this sickness and fighting for the dignity and rights of the poor. They are an inspiration to all who believe in the fight for social justice. Through the Dolores Huerta Foundation, Dolores continues to fight for fair and equal treatment for all people. Can we make our world a better place? Dolores says, "*¡Sí, se puede!* Yes, we can!" You can find out more about Dolores Huerta's continuing work at www.doloreshuerta.org.

*Direct quote from "Education of the Heart—Cesar Chavez in His Own Words," http://www.ufw.org.

Nota para los padres de familia y los maestros

Tanto Dolores Huerta como César Chávez conocieron la injusticia desde muy pequeños y ambos decidieron hacer algo al respecto. Dolores Huerta nació en 1930 en el pueblo minero de Dawson, Nuevo México. Sus padres, Alicia Chávez y Juan Fernández, fueron sus primeros modelos de activismo político. A novecientos millas, en Yuma, Arizona, nació César Chávez en 1927, el hijo de una pareja de campesinos que se quedó sin casa porque no tenía con qué pagar los impuestos.

Dolores y César se conocieron cuando trabajaban con Fred Ross y la Organización de Servicio a la Comunidad (CSO por sus siglas en inglés), un grupo activista de California. En 1962, establecieron la Asociación Nacional de Trabajadores Agrícolas para dedicarse a organizar a los campesinos migratorios de California. Este fue el comienzo de una estrecha y duradera colaboración. En 1967, Dolores y César cofundaron el Sindicato de Trabajadores Agrícolas. César fue nombrado presidente del sindicato y Dolores vicepresidenta. Ese mismo año, César Chávez encabezó una marcha histórica desde Delano, California, hasta los escalones del capitolio en Sacramento, donde miles de seguidores se unieron a él un Domingo de Pascua. Dolores organizó el Boicot Nacional de la Uva y jugó un papel decisivo en la aprobación de la ley de inmigración de 1986, que permitió a más de un millón de trabajadores convertirse en ciudadanos estadounidenses. César y Dolores celebraron juntos muchas victorias en su lucha pacífica por la justicia social, al esforzarse por conseguir beneficios de salud, clínicas y pensiones para los campesinos, y el poder para negociar convenios colectivos.

Fue en Phoenix, Arizona, donde Dolores Huerta por primera vez pronunció la célebre frase "¡Sí, se puede!" mientras se dirigía a un grupo de trabajadores que repetía: "Aquí no es posible organizar a los trabajadores. ¡No se puede! Dolores respondió: "¡Sí, se puede!" Finalmente los trabajadores la escucharon y tuvieron fe.

César Chávez dijo una vez: "Cuando el hombre que alimenta al mundo labrando la tierra se ve privado de los derechos básicos de alimentar, albergar y cuidar a su familia, toda la humanidad se halla enferma". César Chávez y Dolores Huerta dedicaron sus vidas a curar esta enfermedad y a luchar por la dignidad y los derechos de los pobres. Son una inspiración para todos los que creen en la lucha por la justicia social. A través de la Fundación Dolores Huerta, Dolores continúa luchando para que a todos se les trate con justicia e igualdad. ¿Podemos lograr que nuestro mundo sea un lugar mejor? Dolores dice: "¡Sí, se puede!" Para obtener más información acerca del trabajo que Dolores Huerta continúa realizando, visita www.doloreshuerta.org.*

**Cita tomada directamente de "Education of the Heart—Cesar Chavez in His Own Words" (La educación del corazón, César Chávez en sus propias palabras), http://www.ufw.org.*

Photo © Arthur Schatz / Time & Life Pictures / Getty Images

"Cesar was a very smart person and a very hard worker who believed in helping people and reaching goals through nonviolent and peaceful methods." —*Dolores Huerta*

"César era una persona extremadamente inteligente y trabajadora que creía en ayudar a la gente, en alcanzar metas por medio de métodos no violentos, y en la paz." —*Dolores Huerta*

Jaguars slip through the shadows on silent paws. Their spots help them hide. When a jaguar gets close to its prey, it pounces and bites it with powerful jaws.

3:00 A.M.

Nighttime is busy along rain forest rivers and streams. An anaconda lurks at the water's edge. It waits for a deer, capybara, or another animal to come for a drink. The huge snake will grab its prey, squeeze it to death, and swallow it whole.

Anacondas can grow to be 30 feet (91 meters) long.

On the other side of the river, capybaras splash and look for water plants. They eat and rest all through the night. When morning comes they settle down to sleep for the day.

6:00 A.M.

The sky grows light, and nighttime animals get ready to rest. Bats fold their wings, the ocelot and jaguar curl up for a nap, and the armadillo goes back into its burrow. Daytime animals open their eyes and start a new day.

Cricka, cricka! call the toucans. Monkeys chatter. Lizards and snakes climb on forest branches.

Every day and every night, animals find food, water, and safe places to rest in the Amazon rain forest. It provides them with everything they need.

What Is a Tropical Rain Forest?

A tropical rain forest is a thick forest where rain falls nearly every day. The trees grow tall. The climate is warm year-round.

The tall trees form a roof-like canopy that may be 100 feet (30 m) above the ground. A few scattered trees may reach heights of 150 feet (46 m). The canopy is home to amphibians, reptiles, birds, and mammals. Some live their entire lives in the canopy, without ever touching the ground.

Branches of the rain forest trees are covered with plants. Ferns, mosses, bromeliads, and orchids grow there. Bromeliads have a large tank of water at the base of their leaves. Many insects, spiders, frogs, and salamanders live in bromeliads.

The forest floor is covered with a thick layer of fallen leaves called leaf litter. Insects, rodents, frogs, snakes, and other animals live on the forest floor.

Throughout the day and night, animals are busy in the rain forest. Diurnal animals are active during the day. Nocturnal animals are active at night. Which animals in this book are diurnal? Which are nocturnal? Where do they live in the rain forest?

Where Can You Find Tropical Rain Forests?

Tropical rain forests are found in Central and South America, Africa, Asia, and Australia. Most are near the equator. The Amazon rain forest in South America is the biggest rain forest in the world.

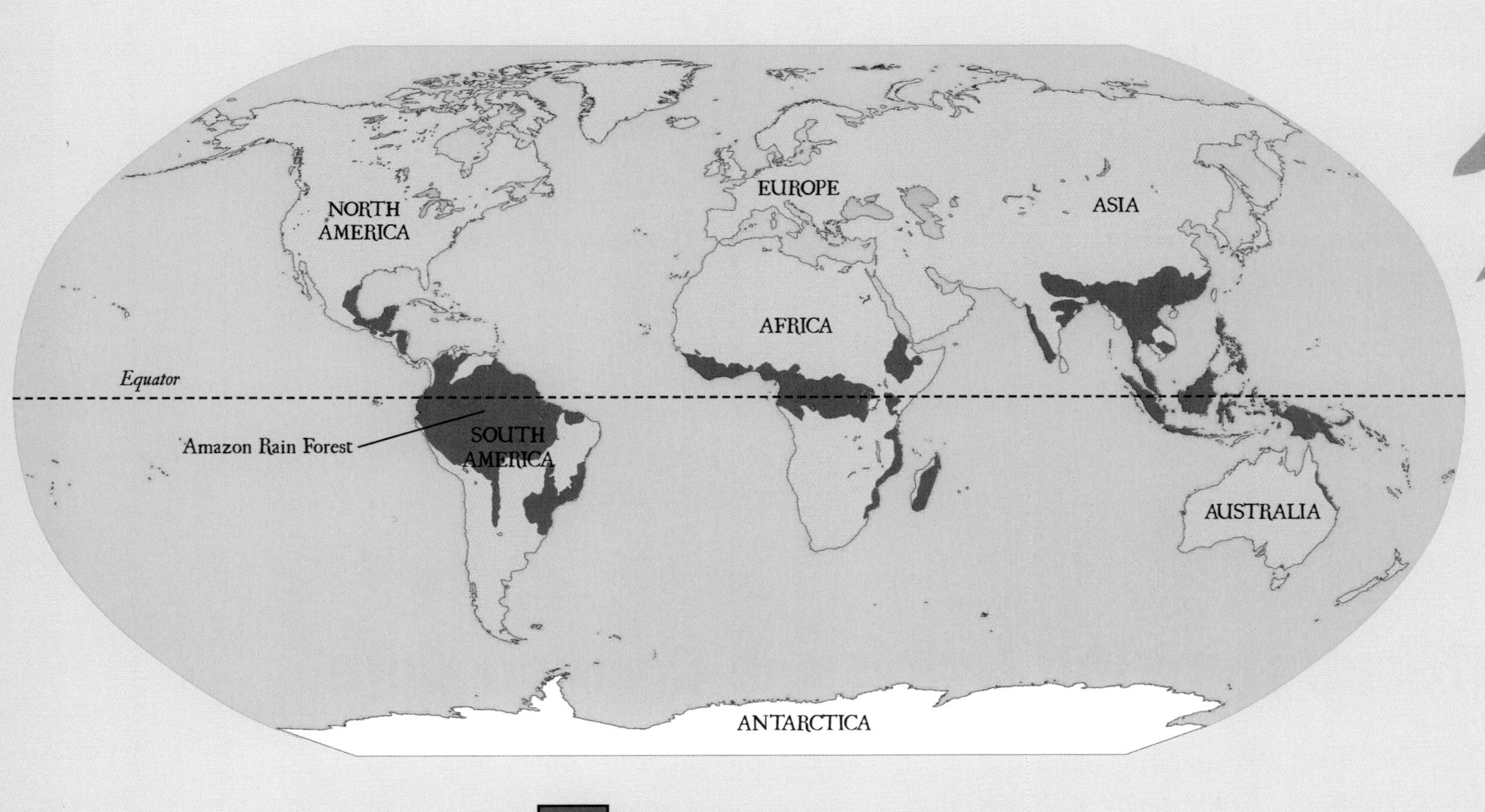

Fun Facts

- Iguanas can grow up to 6.5 feet (2 m) long. They are among the largest lizards in the rain forest.
- Adult emerald tree boas are green, just like their name suggests. But the young snakes are orange. They change color as they grow.
- Sloths have extra bones in their necks. The bones allow the sloths to swivel their heads almost completely around.
- "Armadillo" is a Spanish word that means "little armored one." Bony plates cover the armadillo's body and protect it from predators.
- Owl monkeys are also called night monkeys. They are the only nocturnal monkeys in the Americas.
- Tapirs often live near rivers and are good swimmers. Sometimes they walk underwater along the river bottom and feed.
- Anacondas can weigh more than 220 pounds (100 kilograms). They are the world's heaviest snakes.
- Capybaras are the world's largest rodents. They are about the size of a bulldog. Capybaras are excellent swimmers and can even sleep in the water.

Critical Thinking Using the Common Core

1. Describe how the passing of time is shown throughout this book. (Integration of Knowledge and Ideas)
2. Name three diurnal predators in the Amazon rain forest and their prey. Then name three nocturnal predators and their prey. (Key Ideas and Details)

Glossary

amphibian—an animal that lives in the water when it is young and can live on land as an adult; frogs and salamanders are amphibians

bromeliad—(broh-MEE-lee-ad) a type of tropical plant usually with stiff leaves; some bromeliads get food and water from the air and rain instead of through roots

burrow—a tunnel or hole in the ground made or used by an animal for shelter

canopy—a cover formed by the highest layer of branches and leaves in a forest

climate—average weather of a place throughout the year

diurnal—active during the day

equator—an imaginary line around the middle of Earth

habitat—the natural home or environment of an animal, plant, or other living thing

mammal—an animal that makes its own heat, breathes air, and has hair or fur; female mammals feed milk to their young

nocturnal—active at night

predator—an animal that hunts other animals for food

prey—an animal hunted by another animal for food

reptile—an animal whose body temperature changes with its surroundings; most reptiles lay eggs and have scaly skin; snakes, turtles, and alligators are reptiles

rodent—a mammal with long front teeth used for gnawing; rats, mice, and squirrels are rodents

talon—a long, sharp claw of a bird

troop—a group

Read More

Aloian, Molly, and Bobbie Kalman. *A Rainforest Habitat.* Introducing Habitats. New York: Crabtree Publishing, 2007.

Ganeri, Anita. *Capybara.* A Day in the Life: Rain Forest Animals. Chicago: Heinemann, 2011.

Simon, Seymour. *Tropical Rainforests.* New York: HarperCollins, 2010.

Index

armadillos, 10, 18, 22
bats, 12, 18
birds, 2, 5, 9, 19, 20
capybaras, 16, 17, 22
coatis, 6, 7
daytime, 2–10, 18, 19, 20
deer, 14, 16
frogs, 6–7, 20
iguanas, 4, 22
insects, 6, 7, 10, 12, 13, 20
jaguars, 14, 15, 18
map, 21
monkeys, 2, 3, 13, 19, 22
nighttime, 10–19, 20, 22
ocelots, 11, 18
plants, 17, 20
sloths, 8–9, 22
snakes, 5, 16, 19, 22
tapirs, 14, 22
tarantulas, 14

Internet Sites

FactHound offers a safe, fun way to find Internet sites related to this book. All of the sites on FactHound have been researched by our staff.

Here's all you do:

Visit *www.facthound.com*

Type in this code: 9781479560745

Check out projects, games and lots more at **www.capstonekids.com**

Thanks to our advisers for their expertise, research, and advice:

Janalee P. Caldwell, Curator Emeritus & Professor Emeritus, Biology
Sam Noble Museum, University of Oklahoma

Terry Flaherty, PhD, Professor of English
Minnesota State University, Mankato

Editor: Jill Kalz
Designer: Lori Bye
Art Director: Nathan Gassman
Production Specialist: Kathy McColley
The illustrations in this book were created with cut paper.
Design Elements: Shutterstock/Alfondo de Tomas (map), Alvaro Cabrera Jimenez

Picture Window Books are published by Capstone,
1710 Roe Crest Drive, North Mankato, Minnesota 56003
www.capstonepub.com

Library of Congress Cataloging-in-Publication Data
Arnold, Caroline, author, illustrator.
A day and night in the rain forest / written and illustrated by Caroline Arnold.
pages cm.—(Nonfiction picture books. Caroline Arnold's habitats)
Summary: "Highlights the activities of animals in the Amazon rain forest during one average 24-hour period"—Provided by publisher
Audience: K to grade 3.
Includes bibliographical references and index.
ISBN 978-1-4795-6074-5 (library binding)
ISBN 978-1-4795-6086-8 (paperback)
ISBN 978-1-4795-6146-9 (eBook PDF)
1. Rain forest animals—Behavior—Amazon River Region—Juvenile literature. 2. Rain forest animals—Amazon River Region—Juvenile literature. 3. Rain forests—Amazon River Region—Juvenile literature. 4. Amazon River Region—Juvenile literature. I. Title.
QL112.A77 2015
591.73409861'6—dc23 2014025335

Look for all the books in the series:

Printed in the United States of America in North Mankato 092014 008482CGS15